THIS WALKER BOOK BELONGS TO:

Aiden

laughing

aching

pushing

pouring

chatting

hopping

sulking

kissing

sneezing

hammering

pretending

dribbling

swinging

chatting

blowing

building

resting

catching

For Brenda

First published 1994 by Walker Books Ltd
87 Vauxhall Walk, London SE11 5HJ

This edition published 2006 for Index Books Ltd

2 4 6 8 10 9 7 5 3 1

© 1994 Shirley Hughes

The right of Shirley Hughes to be identified as
author/illustrator of this work has been asserted by her in
accordance with the Copyright, Designs and Patents Act 1988

This book has been typeset in Plantin

Printed in China

All rights reserved. No part of this book may be reproduced, transmitted
or stored in an information retrieval system in any form or by any means, graphic,
electronic or mechanical, including photocopying, taping and recording,
without prior written permission from the publisher.

British Library Cataloguing in Publication Data:
a catalogue record for this book is available from the British Library

ISBN 1-84428-529-4

www.walkerbooks.co.uk

Chatting

Shirley Hughes

WALKER BOOKS
AND SUBSIDIARIES
LONDON • BOSTON • SYDNEY • AUCKLAND

I like chatting.

I chat to the cat,

and I chat in the car.

I chat with friends in the park,

and to the lady at the supermarket.

Grown-ups like chatting too.

Sometimes these chats go on
for rather a long time.

The lady next door is
an especially good chatterer.

When Mum is busy she says that there
are just too many chatterboxes around.

So I go off and chat to Bemily –
but she never says a word.

Olly likes

a chat on his

toy telephone.

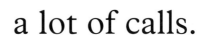

He makes

a lot of calls.

But I can chat
to Grandma
and Grandpa
on the real
telephone.

Some of the best chats
of all are with Dad,

when he comes to
say good night.

laughing

aching

pushing

pouring

chatting

hopping

sulking

kissing

sneezing

hammering

pretending

dribbling

swinging

chatting

blowing

building

resting

catching

WALKER BOOKS is the world's leading
independent publisher of children's books.
Working with the best authors and illustrators
we create books for all ages, from babies
to teenagers – books your child will
grow up with and always remember. So…

FOR THE BEST CHILDREN'S BOOKS,
LOOK FOR THE BEAR